Flicker's Round Trip

Treasure wildlife!
Ann Hanson

Flicker's
Round Trip

Ann Hanson

Paper Jam Publishing
Eastsound • WA

Flicker's Round Trip

Paper Jam Publishing
PO Box 435
Eastsound, WA 98245

Library of Congress Control Number: 2003103425

Children • Pacific Northwest • Flickers

ISBN 1-888345-51-9

First Edition

Foreword

Flicker's Round Trip is a true story. As a volunteer at Wolf Hollow Wildlife Rehabilitation Center on San Juan Island, I helped a young flicker who had fallen from the nest. For three months I cared for him, encouraging him to eat and grow. When he became an adult, my husband and I took him on the ferryboat back to Orcas Island. We released him on Mountain Lake Trail, near where he had been found. The idea for this story came to me as he flew up into the woods where he had hatched. It was a joy to return him to the wild—to take him home. Every time we walk that trail, I listen for flicker calls, and when I hear one, I smile.

I have great respect for the work Wolf Hollow does. A portion of the proceeds from every copy of this book that is sold will go to Wolf Hollow Wildlife Rehabilitation Center.

Ann Hanson

KerPlop! Flicker landed flat on his back in the dirt on Mountain Lake Trail. He was no bigger than a bar of soap—just a few straggly feathers and a little sharp beak. Many people wouldn't even have noticed the little woodpecker there on the ground.

Do you see him?

Flicker was lucky. A hiker spotted him just as two big black-and-brown dogs came bounding up. Big dogs play too roughly for baby birds. The hiker put Flicker in his lunch sack for safety. Flicker couldn't see much, but the light came golden through the brown paper. It was like the light at sunset when baby birds get sleepy. Flicker's eyes blinked twice and closed.

Flicker woke up when he was carried onto the big ferryboat, Illahee. He could hear cars driving onto the boat, doors slamming, and lots of loud talking. The ferryboat's hoarse "Toot! Tooooot!" scared Flicker, but soon the steady thrum of the big engines lulled him back to sleep.

Can you find the brown lunch bag on the ferryboat?

When Flicker woke up, gentle hands were checking to see if he was hurt. He wasn't. He was just very small and very young, and he didn't have all of his feathers yet. He was given a little cage at Wolf Hollow, a hospital for wild animals and birds.

Someone offered Flicker food. He had a terrible time eating. He was very hungry! But he was so excited he kept jerking his head and knocking the berries and cat food out of the tweezers. He got more food on the outside of his tummy than he did on the inside. What a mess! Flicker also couldn't stop talking. He even talked with his mouth full. Perhaps that's just the way all little flickers are.

Have you ever talked with your mouth full, like Flicker?

One day Flicker noticed the little swallows in the next cage. They sat with their beaks gaping wide as soon as they saw the tweezers full of food. Flicker watched them and learned to wait with his beak open too, but he never learned to sit still and he never learned to be quiet. After a while, he began to get more food into his tummy, and people started to say, "Good little Flicker." And Flicker began to grow.

How many baby swallows do you see?

Soon Flicker was moved into a larger cage. This one had a perch that looked like a tree stump. Flicker could hide behind it and poke his head up over the top to see what was going on. Flicker seemed to be playing peek-a-boo.

Did you ever play that game when you were little?

Before long, Flicker grew so big that he was moved outside to a room-sized cage called an aviary. He still jabbered all day long. Now he could stretch his growing wings and fly from branch to branch. People offered him food from tweezers, but more and more often Flicker fed himself from the berries and cat food they had left. They brought him meal worms too, which he especially liked.

Would you like to eat Flicker's food?

Flicker had so much to look at from his big cage. He could see the sky and

the woods and feel the breezes and the warm sun on his feathers. He heard a barred owl call out, "Whoo, whoo," from another aviary. He saw someone take pans of food and water out to the raccoon cage, and he could just glimpse a little fox peeking around the corner of his house.

Flicker could see a great blue heron all wrapped up in a bright bandage. Someone brought fish to the heron for its breakfast and again for its dinner. The heron had a long neck, much longer than Flicker's neck. It had long legs, too, and a long beak.

What does the heron have in his beak?

Flicker saw people take fish to the baby otters and the baby seals. He could watch the seal pups splashing and diving in their swimming pool, and learning to catch fish. Nobody brought fish to him. Flickers don't eat fish. Flicker ate his cat food and his berries and worms, and he grew and grew. He grew and grew until he was all grown up. Finally the people at Wolf Hollow said Flicker was ready to go back home to the woods by Mountain Lake.

Flicker rode on the ferryboat again, this time in a cardboard pet carrier. He was much too big for a lunch sack! He was about the size of a whole loaf of bread. He didn't fall asleep, either. He amused himself by hammering on the cardboard carrier and poking his sharp beak out through the air holes.

Then Flicker was being carried along Mountain Lake Trail. Swaying in his carrier, he faintly remembered his ride in the lunch sack. This time the carrier was set down by the trail and the top was opened wide. Flicker popped his head up and shouted, "Cheee-ew!"

Flicker spread his wings and flew right up into a big fir tree. He was free to live his life as a wild bird in the forest, as all flickers should. He could hear the gentle gurgle of the lake water and the soft shoosh of the breeze in the tree branches. A raven croaked hoarsely out over the water. A winter wren sang cheerfully in the brush below.

"Cheee-ew," called Flicker from way up high. There he was—a dark flicker shape against a gray swirl of cloud. Flicker's round trip was over. He was home.

Author's Note

The flicker of the story is a northern flicker, *Colaptes aurata*, of which there are two sub-species. The yellow-shafted flicker occurs more often in the east, the red-shafted more often in the west. The two often crossbreed on the Great Plains and in western Canada, where the populations overlap. That accounts for the color variations we see in individual birds. Note that flickers have four toes on each foot. They cling to tree trunks using their strong tail feathers to support them. Their sturdy black beaks hammer on the trees, catching bugs in the bark. Their barred wings and speckled chests help them blend with the forest trees.

Ann Hanson is a native of Bellingham, Washington. She taught high school German and English for many years before she retired and could devote her time to painting. She has taken workshops with Steve Mayo, Caroline Buchanan, Jan Kunz, Carol Merrick, Frank Loudin, and Charles Mulvey. She paints with The Daubers in Bellingham and The Pallettes on Orcas Island. Her work is shown at the Orcas Island Artworks, and her paintings, calendars, and cards are sold throughout Washington and Oregon. Writing and illustrating *Flicker's Round Trip* provided a creative opportunity for Ann to bring her experience in wildlife rehabilitation to a young audience.